THE PADAWAN MENACE

ADAPTED BY ACE LANDERS
BASED ON THE SCREENPLAY BY MICHAEL PRICE

SCHOLASTIC INC.
NEW YORK   TORONTO   LONDON   AUCKLAND
SYDNEY   MEXICO CITY   NEW DELHI   HONG KONG

AS THE CLONE WARS RAGED ACROSS THE GALAXY, A GROUP OF PADAWANS WERE ON A CLASS FIELD TRIP . . .

. . . BUT THEIR REAL ADVENTURE WAS ABOUT TO BEGIN.

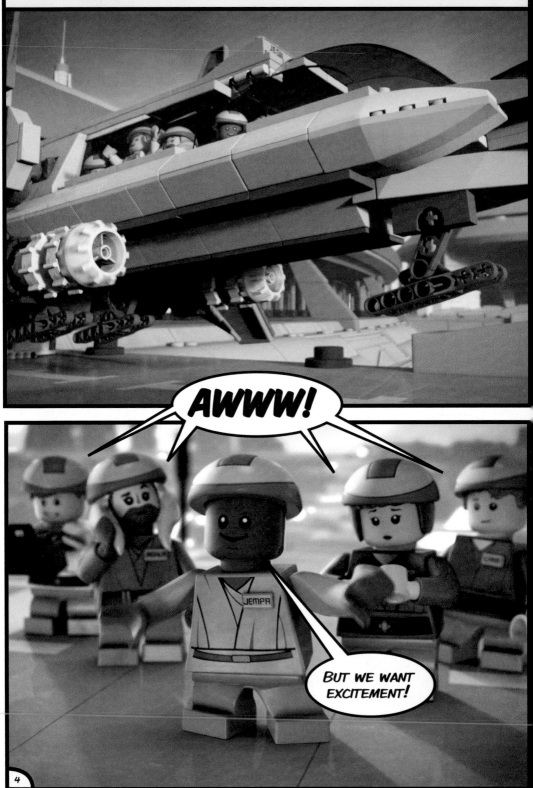

AWWW!

BUT WE WANT EXCITEMENT!

4

TWO DROIDS NAMED C-3PO AND R2-D2 WERE THE GROUP'S SPECIAL TOUR GUIDES.

SUDDENLY, YODA FELT A DISTURBANCE IN THE FORCE.

LEAVE YOU, I MUST. A GRAVE THREAT TO THE REPUBLIC, I FEAR.

YODA HURRIED INTO THE SENATE AND LEFT THE DROIDS TO WATCH THE PADAWANS.

WAIT! I'M A PROTOCOL DROID, NOT A SUBSTITUTE TEACHER! PUT ME DOWN!

5

THE PADAWANS FINALLY PUT C-3PO DOWN AND BEGAN THE TOUR.

AS THE GROUP ENTERED THE SENATE, A MYSTERIOUS BOY SPIED ON THEM.

THIS SURE BEATS THAT ORPHANAGE!

6

THE BOY SNEAKED PAST THE GUARDS . . .

. . . BY PRETENDING TO BE A PADAWAN.

SENATE CHAMBER

HEY, WHERE DID THAT KID GO?

AWESOME!

IAN

7

IAN WASN'T THE ONLY ONE HIDING. ASAJJ VENTRESS, AN EVIL SEPARATIST AGENT, STOOD IN THE SHADOWS.

ASAJJ CALLED DARTH SIDIOUS TO SHARE SOME NEWS.

I HAVE STOLEN THE REPUBLIC'S SECRET BATTLE PLANS.

YOU HAVE DONE WELL, VENTRESS.

9

INSIDE A POD IN THE GALACTIC SENATE, ONE PADAWAN NOTICED THE NEW KID.

I DON'T REMEMBER YOU, IAN.

BOBBY

YES, YOU DOOOO. . . .

IAN

EVERYONE KNOWS THAT JEDI MIND TRICKS DON'T WORK ON JEDI — EVEN WHEN THEY'RE PADAWANS!

THE GUARDS WERE STILL LOOKING FOR IAN. HE TRIED TO ESCAPE BY REWIRING THE PADAWANS' SENATE POD.

THE ESCAPE DID NOT GO WELL.

YEEAAHHH!

AAAAHHH!

HOLD ON!

MEANWHILE, YODA HAD FOUND THE DISTURBANCE IN THE FORCE. IT WAS ASAJJ.

TIRED OF BEING RIGHT EVERY TIME, I AM.

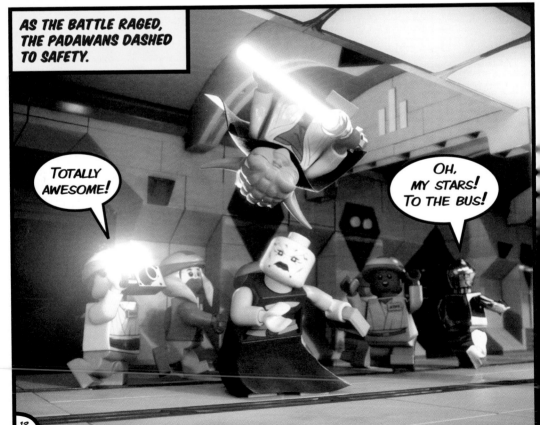

AS THE BATTLE RAGED, THE PADAWANS DASHED TO SAFETY.

TOTALLY AWESOME!

OH, MY STARS! TO THE BUS!

12

WHILE YODA AND ASAJJ DUELED, A BATTLE DROID ESCAPED WITH THE SECRET BATTLE PLANS.

USING THE FORCE, YODA TRAPPED THE EVIL ASAJJ . . .

. . . AND CHASED AFTER THE BATTLE DROID WITH CLONE COMMANDER CODY.

SECRET BATTLE PLANS, THAT DROID HAS!

I'M ON IT!

THE PADAWANS ESCAPED TO THE BUS — BUT THERE WAS NO DRIVER!

LUCKILY, R2 COULD FLY THE SHIP.

I CAN'T FLY THIS THING!

THE BATTLE DROID BLASTED OFF WITH THE STOLEN PLANS.

YODA AND CODY JUMPED INTO THE CLOSEST SPACESHIP.

FOLLOW HIM, WE MUST!

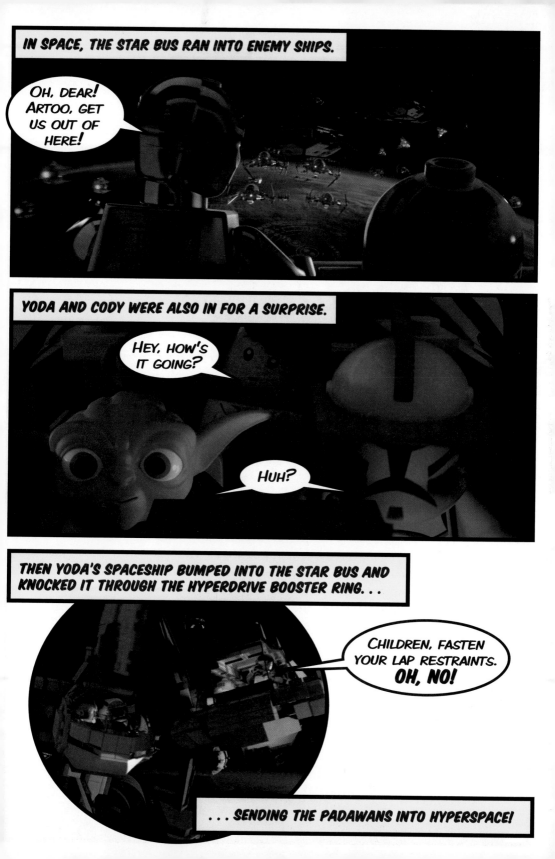

IN SPACE, THE STAR BUS RAN INTO ENEMY SHIPS.

OH, DEAR! ARTOO, GET US OUT OF HERE!

YODA AND CODY WERE ALSO IN FOR A SURPRISE.

HEY, HOW'S IT GOING?

HUH?

THEN YODA'S SPACESHIP BUMPED INTO THE STAR BUS AND KNOCKED IT THROUGH THE HYPERDRIVE BOOSTER RING...

CHILDREN, FASTEN YOUR LAP RESTRAINTS. OH, NO!

...SENDING THE PADAWANS INTO HYPERSPACE!

THE STAR BUS CAME OUT OF HYPERSPACE AND CRASH-LANDED ON TATOOINE.

GSSSHH!

AWESOME!

YAY! LET'S DO THAT AGAIN!

BUT THE SHIP WAS DAMAGED IN THE CRASH. THE PADAWANS WERE STRANDED!

LOOK AT OUR SHIP! HOW COULD YOU LET THIS HAPPEN?

BLURP!

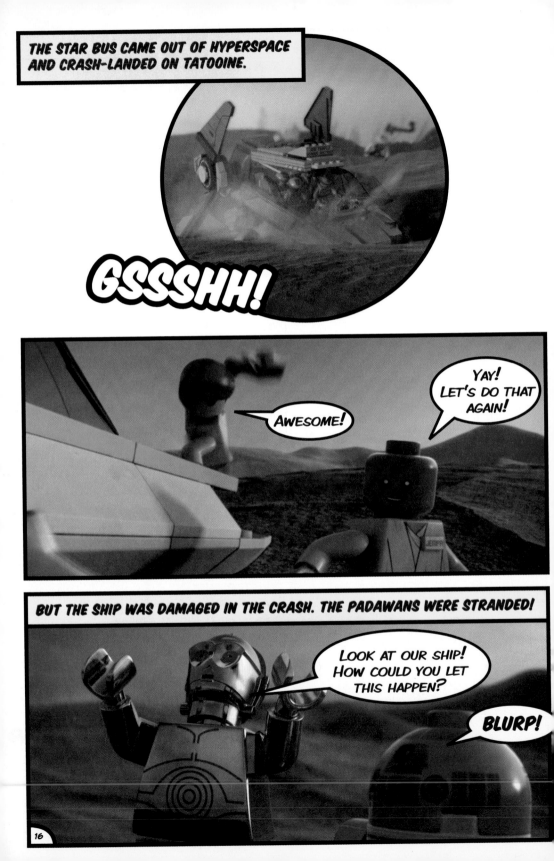

16

MEANWHILE, YODA CHASED THE BATTLE DROID TO THE ICE PLANET HOTH.

TRACK THAT DROID THROUGH THE SNOW, WE MUST.

I'VE GOT A BAD FEELING ABOUT THIS.

17

CODY AND YODA SPLIT UP TO SEARCH FOR THE DROID.

HOW OLD ARE YOU, A MILLION?

TO KNOW MORE THAN YOU, OLD ENOUGH I AM, HMM!

AT LEAST KNOW HOW TO TALK NORMAL, I DO.

18

BACK ON TATOOINE, C-3PO, R2-D2, AND THE PADAWANS LOOKED FOR A NEW SHIP.

YOU YOUNGLINGS STAY HERE WHILE I FIND A PILOT IN THIS CANTINA. **DON'T TOUCH ANYTHING!**

BUT THE YOUNGLINGS HAD OTHER PLANS.

19

WHEN C-3PO RAN TO STOP THEM . . .

GREAT BANTHA BREATH! WHAT ARE YOU DOING!

. . . HE ACCIDENTALLY KNOCKED DOWN A WALL.

OH, MY! I'M TERRIBLY SORRY, MASTER JABBA.

JABBA THE HUTT WAS NOT HAPPY.

20

ON HOTH, YODA AND IAN WERE STILL SEARCHING FOR THE BATTLE DROID. THEY WERE GETTING COLD.

TO KEEP WARM, STICK OUR HEADS IN THIS ANIMAL'S GUTS WILL WE.

GROSS!

SUDDENLY, THE BATTLE DROID LEAPED OUT OF THE TAUNTAUN! YODA STRUCK IT DOWN WITH HIS LIGHTSABER.

WHOA! SECRET BATTLE PLANS! THAT WAS EASY!

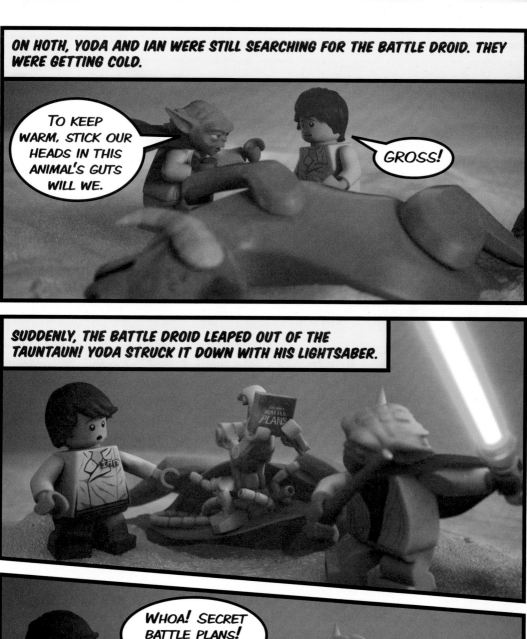

21

BUT IAN SPOKE TOO SOON. DROIDEKAS SURROUNDED THEM.

BLAST THEM!

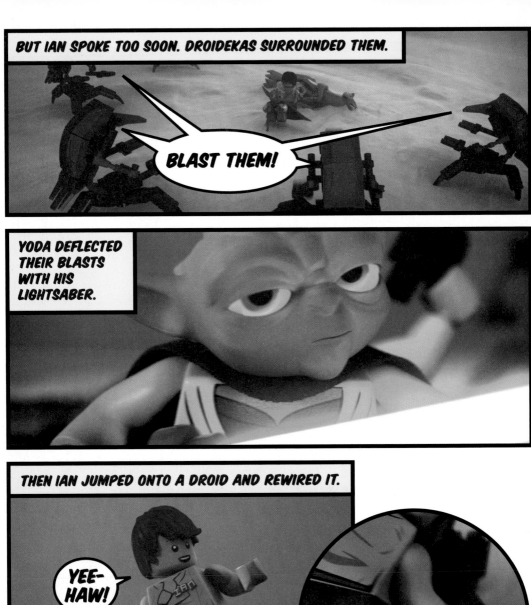

YODA DEFLECTED THEIR BLASTS WITH HIS LIGHTSABER.

THEN IAN JUMPED ONTO A DROID AND REWIRED IT.

YEE-HAW!

22

IAN AND YODA GALLOPED BACK TO THEIR SHIP.

AW MAN, THE SHIP IS BROKEN!

YODA USED THE FORCE TO CREATE A NEW ONE.

23

IAN AND YODA JUMPED INTO THE SPACESHIP AND BLASTED OFF WITH THE SECRET PLANS.

BUT THEIR MISSION WASN'T OVER. THEY RECEIVED A DISTRESS CALL.

MASTER YODA, THE YOUNGLINGS ARE IN DANGER!

RESCUE THEM, WE WILL.

ON TATOOINE, JABBA WAS SPEAKING TO A CROWD OF CREATURES. C-3PO TRANSLATED HIS ORDERS.

DOPA DROI WAMMA JABBA!

THESE DROIDS WILL PAY FOR INSULTING JABBA BY FIGHTING EACH OTHER . . . ?!

OH, MY! I DON'T WANT TO FIGHT MY BEST FRIEND!

C-3PO RUSHED OVER TO THE PADAWANS, WHO WERE LOCKED BEHIND BARS.

I'M SO SORRY! I'M A FAILURE!

BUT AGAIN, THE YOUNGLINGS HAD OTHER PLANS.

YOU'RE NOT A FAILURE. YOU'RE A HERO! BREAK THOSE PILLARS WITH YOUR WEAPON!

C-3PO BROKE THE PILLARS, AND THE ROOF CRASHED DOWN ON JABBA.

THEN R2-D2 FREED THE PADAWANS!

BEFORE THEY COULD ESCAPE, A FEROCIOUS RANCOR RUSHED OUT OF THE PALACE!

IT HEADED STRAIGHT FOR THE PADAWANS!

RUN AWAY!

JABBA'S PALACE

27

SUDDENLY, A GIANT MAGNET PICKED UP C-3PO. IT WAS YODA AND IAN, COMING TO THE RESCUE!

WHOA!

THE PADAWANS GRABBED ONTO C-3PO, AND THE SHIP LIFTED THEM INTO THE SKY. THE YOUNGLINGS WERE SAVED!

WELCOME JABBA's PALACE

YODA, IAN, C-3PO, R2-D2, AND THE PADAWANS HEADED BACK TO THE JEDI TEMPLE.

I AM A HERO! I ONLY WISH MASTER YODA COULD SEE ME NOW.

SEE YOU I COULD, IF SITTING ON ME YOU WERE NOT.

EXCUSE ME, SIR!

WHEN THEY ARRIVED, THERE WAS A BIG CELEBRATION FOR IAN AND THE BRAVE PADAWANS.

YODA GAVE IAN A MEDAL OF HONOR.

MANY ADVENTURES IN YOUR FUTURE HAVE YOU, YOUNG IAN.

30

THANKS, BUT MY NAME IS NOT IAN — IT'S HAN . . . HAN SOLO.

HAN

A PLEASURE TO MEET YOU, MASTER SOLO.

THANKS, GOLDYPANTS.

HAN

ALL WAS WELL AGAIN IN THE REPUBLIC.

AWESOME!